Invisible
Ivan

Maverick

Chapter Readers

'Invisible Ivan'
An original concept by Katie Dale
© Katie Dale

Illustrated by Max Rambaldi

Published by MAVERICK ARTS PUBLISHING LTD

Studio 11, City Business Centre, 6 Brighton Road,

Horsham, West Sussex, RH13 5BB

© Maverick Arts Publishing Limited February 2021

+44 (0)1403 256941

A CIP catalogue record for this book is available at the British Library.

ISBN 978-1-84886-781-9

www.maverickbooks.co.uk

This book is rated as: Lime Band (Guided Reading)

Invisible Ivan

written by **Katie Dale**

Illustrated by **Max Rambaldi**

Chapter 1

Ivan loved visiting Great-Aunt Polly and her dog, Geronimo.

"Woof! Woof! WOOF!" Geronimo barked excitedly as Ivan threw his ball for him.

"Geronimo loves playing with you," Great-Aunt Polly smiled. "I'm afraid I'm too old to play with him now."

"But not too old for pranks?" Ivan asked.

Great-Aunt Polly's eyes twinkled. "You're *never* too old for pranks!" she chuckled.

Ivan and his mum laughed. Great-Aunt Polly might be very old and slow, but she knew more tricks than anyone in Ivan's class, and she was filled with fun and mischief from her twinkly eyes down to her fluffy leopard-print slippers.

"What trick shall we learn today, Great-Aunt Polly?" Ivan asked excitedly.

Great-Aunt Polly grinned. "Secret messages!" she whispered. "I just need to find my glasses..."

"You haven't lost them again, have you?" Ivan's mum frowned.

"Yes!" Great-Aunt Polly chuckled as she looked around. "Don't worry, they'll be here somewhere..."

Ivan and his mum helped her search. It was

so strange that Great-Aunt Polly could remember

hundreds of pranks from when she was a child,

but she could never remember where she'd left

things like glasses or keys!

"Here they are!" Ivan cried, spotting them in Geronimo's dog-basket.

"What are they doing there?" Great-Aunt Polly giggled. "How strange!"

Ivan laughed. But his mum didn't. She looked worried. "Are you sure you're okay to look after Ivan this afternoon, Aunt Polly?" she asked.

"Of course!" Great-Aunt Polly laughed. "See you later, dear! Ivan and I are going to have great fun together, aren't we?"

"Definitely!" Ivan grinned.

Chapter 2

Ivan waved goodbye to his mum, then he played with Geronimo until the little dog fell asleep.

"Come on, Ivan," Great-Aunt Polly whispered, leading him to the kitchen. "Time to make some invisible ink!"

She mixed baking soda and water in a big bowl. Then she dipped a paintbrush into the mixture and carefully wrote an invisible message on a piece of paper.

"I can't see anything!" Ivan frowned.

Great-Aunt Polly smiled. She showed him how
to reveal the message by holding the paper over
a lamp, or painting it with grape juice.

"It's like magic!" Ivan gasped, as the hidden
words appeared.

Great-Aunt Polly beamed. "Now we can write secret messages to each other!"

Ivan grinned. He couldn't wait to write his own secret message. He picked up the paintbrush and swirled it in the big bowl of ink thoughtfully.

BANG!

A ball slammed into the kitchen window, making Ivan jump—and knock the bowl over! Oh no! The invisible ink spilled all over Ivan!

Ivan gasped as his fingers and arms began to disappear. He was turning invisible!

Chapter 3

Ivan couldn't believe his eyes. His whole body had completely vanished!

Great-Aunt Polly's eyes widened. "Oh my goodness! I had no idea invisible ink worked on people!"

"This is amazing!" Ivan grinned. "Think of all the pranks I can do now!"

"True!" Great-Aunt Polly laughed. "And don't

worry, grape juice should turn you visible again."

Just then, they heard a girl's voice outside. "Please can you throw my football back?" she called.

Ivan looked out the window and saw a little girl peering over the garden fence.

Great-Aunt Polly's eyes twinkled. "Follow me, Ivan," she whispered.

She walked slowly out of the back door, leaning on her stick. Ivan followed.

"Oh, I'm afraid I'm far too old to throw footballs," she told the girl. "But luckily, I can do a bit of magic..."

She wiggled her fingers in the direction of the ball. Ivan grinned. He picked up the football, trying not to giggle. The little girl's eyes widened. The ball was floating in mid-air!

Ivan threw the ball back.

As it sailed towards her, the girl ran away, squealing. "Mum!" she cried. "The old lady next-door's magic!"

Great-Aunt Polly and Ivan laughed. Being invisible was GREAT fun!

Chapter 4

Just then, Geronimo started barking.

"Your mum must be back!" Great-Aunt Polly cried. They hurried inside.

"Hello Aunt Polly!" Ivan's mum said, walking into the kitchen, Geronimo at her heels. "Where's Ivan?"

Great-Aunt Polly grinned. "Oh, he's around somewhere…"

Ivan grinned. He tip-toed carefully behind his

mum—and pulled her scarf off!

"What the?!" Ivan's mum cried, picking up

her scarf. "How strange."

"Woof!" Geronimo barked, confused.

Great-Aunt Polly giggled. Ivan's mum put her scarf back on. Ivan pulled it off again.

"Hey!" his mum gasped.

"Woof! Woof!" Geronimo barked, sniffing around.

Ivan struggled not to laugh. This was hilarious! He pulled the scarf off for a third time.

"Woof! Woof! Woof!" Geronimo barked madly.

"What is going on?" Ivan's mum gasped, spinning round quickly, and knocking over the carton of grape juice. "Oh I'm so sorry, Aunt Polly!" she cried, mopping it up and picking up the empty carton.

Ivan froze. Great-Aunt Polly turned pale.

Oh no! Without grape juice, how would Ivan

turn visible again?

Chapter 5

"Ivan!" his mum called, after she'd mopped up the mess. "Where are you? It's time to go!"

Ivan opened his mouth to answer—but Great-Aunt Polly spoke first. "Oh, I remember now," she said quickly. "I sent Ivan to the corner shop to get more grape juice!"

"On his own?" Ivan's mum said crossly. "I'll go and find him."

"I'll come with you," Great-Aunt Polly said.

"No," Ivan's mum said. "You stay here. Call me if Ivan turns up."

"I would..." Great-Aunt Polly said. "But I seem to have lost my phone handset..."

Ivan's mum sighed. "I'll help you find it."

While Ivan's mum searched for the

phone, Great-Aunt Polly quickly dipped a paintbrush in what was left of the invisible ink, and hurriedly wrote a message.

Ivan frowned. How could he read the message without grape juice? Then he remembered he could use a lamp instead. Maybe that would turn him visible again too?

He picked up the paper and hurried to the lounge. Ivan tried standing close to the lamp... but nothing happened. He was still invisible. He sighed. Then he held the paper over the table lamp and a message slowly appeared:

Don't worry. I'll get more grape juice. Sit tight in my bedroom until we're back!

Ivan smiled.

Ivan had never been in Great-Aunt Polly's bedroom before. There were lots of family photos on the wall and a gold watch on her bedside table. Ivan smiled at Great-Aunt Polly's wedding photo. She looked so young!

Suddenly the bedroom door opened and Ivan's mum hurried in.

Ivan held his breath and pressed himself

against the wall as she searched for the phone.

"Losing a phone is one thing," she muttered under her breath. "But losing a child is much worse! I should never have left Ivan alone with her... I won't make that mistake again!"

As she hurried out of the room, Ivan frowned. He loved staying with Great-Aunt Polly! It wasn't her fault he'd spilled the ink all over himself!

He had to tell his mum the truth!

But it was too late. Through the window, he saw his mum's car driving away. Geronimo howled sadly as the car disappeared down the road.

Ivan knew just how he felt.

Chapter 6

Suddenly, Geronimo stopped howling and padded into Great-Aunt Polly's bedroom. He sniffed around for a few minutes, then, to Ivan's surprise, he took Great-Aunt Polly's gold watch off the bedside table! Ivan gasped as the dog ran away with it in his mouth, and disappeared through the dog-flap into the back garden.

Ivan hesitated. Great-Aunt Polly had told him

to stay inside... but what if Geronimo lost her precious watch? Ivan had to follow! Luckily, he was just small enough to crawl through the dog-flap too.

Outside, Ivan spotted Geronimo scampering behind some bushes. What was the dog up to? Ivan hurried after him, and found Geronimo digging a small hole.

Suddenly, he dropped Great-Aunt Polly's watch

in it and began to bury it!

"Geronimo, stop!" Ivan cried.

The dog spun round, confused. When he

couldn't see anyone there, he began to whine.

He picked up the watch in his mouth.

"Geronimo, drop!" Ivan commanded.

The dog immediately dropped the watch and ran away, barking. Just then, Ivan heard a strange sound… it was a phone ringing!

Ivan dug around in the dirt behind the bushes and found Great-Aunt Polly's phone— and some of her other missing things!

He dug up jewellery,

a TV remote

control,

and her keys!

Ivan gasped. Geronimo must have stolen all these things and buried them!

Great-Aunt Polly wasn't getting forgetful after all!

Chapter 7

Just then, Ivan's mum and Great-Aunt Polly returned.

"Where on earth can Ivan be?" his mum said anxiously. "The shop-keeper hadn't seen him!"

"Mum!" Ivan cried, running over. "I'm here!"

"Ivan?" his mum frowned, looking around. "Where are you?"

Oops! Ivan had forgotten he was invisible!

Luckily, Great-Aunt Polly was holding a big carton of grape juice. Ivan grabbed it.

"What the... that carton is flying!" Ivan's mum gasped as the carton flew through the air...

Her eyes widened as Ivan opened it...

Then her jaw dropped as Ivan poured it all over himself—and was suddenly visible again!

"Ivan!" his mum cried. "What happened? Where have you been?"

"I was here the whole time," Ivan explained. "But I accidentally turned myself invisible with invisible ink. I'm sorry I didn't tell you before. I didn't want you to worry."

"Oh Ivan!" his mum cried, hugging him. "Never be afraid to tell me the truth!"

"I'm sorry too," said Great-Aunt Polly. "I thought you might not let me look after Ivan

anymore if you knew my ink turned him invisible."

"Oh Aunt Polly," Ivan's mum said. "It's your memory I'm worried about. You do seem very forgetful these days."

Great-Aunt Polly sighed. "I do keep losing things."

"No!" Ivan cried, grinning. "Great-Aunt Polly isn't forgetful at all—I'll show you!"

Chapter 8

Ivan led them behind the bushes and showed them all the things he'd dug up. Everyone gasped.

"When you were both out I saw Geronimo take Great-Aunt Polly's watch and try to bury it!" Ivan explained. "He must have stolen and buried all these things too!"

"Geronimo?!" Great-Aunt Polly cried.

Geronimo padded over, his tail between his legs.

Ivan stroked him gently. "He looks very sorry, Great-Aunt Polly," he said.

"Oh Geronimo," Great-Aunt Polly sighed. "I'm sorry too."

Ivan and his mum frowned.

"But why?" Ivan's mum cried. "Geronimo's the one who caused all the trouble!"

"Dogs bury things when they get bored or lonely," Great-Aunt Polly explained, stroking Geronimo gently. "I'm getting old. I'm sorry I can't take you for long walks or play football with you anymore, Geronimo. Maybe it's time I gave you to someone who can."

"But... but you can't give Geronimo away!"

Ivan said, hugging him. "You'd miss him too much!

And I'd miss him too. I love playing with him!"

Then he had an idea. "Can we take him home

and look after him, Mum? Then we could bring

him to visit Great-Aunt Polly?"

Ivan's mum shook her head sadly. "I'm sorry, Ivan, but your dad's allergic to dogs."

Everyone looked at Geronimo sadly.

Then Ivan's mum smiled. "But we could come by and look after Geronimo," she suggested. "We only live around the corner so we could visit every day to play with him and take him for long walks. That way he could still live with Aunt Polly."

Ivan's eyes widened. "That would be amazing!"

"But we'd have to promise to walk him every day, rain or shine," Ivan's mum said. "Do you think you can do that, Ivan?"

Ivan thought for a moment, then broke into a

big grin. "Yes! I promise! If that's okay with you,

Great-Aunt Polly?"

Great-Aunt Polly beamed. "That sounds

perfect! What do you think, Geronimo?"

"Woof! Woof! WOOF!" Geronimo barked, his

tail wagging happily.

"That settles it!" Great-Aunt Polly cried.

Everyone laughed.

Discussion Points

1. How did Ivan become invisible in the story?

2. What was your favourite part of the story?

3. What is missing at the beginning, which Ivan, Great-Aunt Polly and Mum have to look for?

4. Who was burying Great-Aunt Polly's things in the back garden?

a) Ivan

b) Mum

c) Geronimo

5. Why do you think Ivan didn't want to tell his mum he was invisible?

6. Who was your favourite character and why?

7. There were moments in the story when things **aren't what they seem**. How does Ivan deal with this?

8. What do you think happens after the end of the story?

Book Bands for Guided Reading

The Institute of Education book banding system is a scale of colours that reflects the various levels of reading difficulty. The bands are assigned by taking into account the content, the language style, the layout and phonics. Word, phrase and sentence level work is also taken into consideration.

The Maverick Readers Scheme is a bright, attractive range of books covering the pink to grey bands. All of these books have been book banded for guided reading to the industry standard and edited by a leading educational consultant.

To view the whole Maverick Readers scheme, visit our website at

www.maverickearlyreaders.com

Or scan the QR code to view our scheme instantly!

Maverick Chapter Readers
(From Lime to Grey Band)

Pink
Red
Yellow
Blue
Green
Orange
Turquoise
Purple
Gold
White
Lime
Brown
Grey